MEL BAY'S

GETTING INTO... CLASSIC GUITAR

by BEN BOLT

www.benboltguitar.com

GW00775887

CD CONTENTS

1	Arpeggios Using Open Strings [1:53]	16	Amador [:53]	31	Saltarello [:36]
2	Tremolo [:20]	17	Gamboa [1:48]	32	Hark the Herald Angels Sing [:47]
3	Right-Hand Studies [3:55]	18	Sosa Hill [:37]	33	O Little Town of Bethlehem [1:03]
4	Classic Chord Progression [:14]	19	Santa Clara [:52]	34	Allegretto [:46]
5	Natural Notes 1st Position [:30]	20	Andante 3/4 [1:57]	35	Hallelujah Chorus [4:28]
6	Military Step [1:11]	21	Andante 4/4 [1:08]	36	A Scale/Alternating Open E String [:12]
7	Point of Reference [:17]	22	Hymn for Zadok [1:11]	37	Dominant Peddler [:26]
8	Pachelbel's Canon [2:03]	23	Streets of Paris [3:22]	38	Study [:45]
9	Double Note Dance [1:31]	24	Spring Morning [1:45]	39	Prelude in A [1:30]
10	Gavotte [3:18]	25	March [:47]	40	Allegretto [1:25]
11	House of the Rising Sun [1:04]	26	March [1:28]	41	Allegretto [1:49]
12	Danza Latino [1:02]	27	Allegretto [1:23]	42	Prelude in E [1:11]
13	Für Elise [:42]	28	Pinky Pivot [:50]	43	Spoof on a French Folk Song [1:35]
14	Anitra's Dance [:51]	29	Away in a Manger [1:16]	44	Study in Sixths [3:23]
15	Balboa [1:11]	30	Allegro Alla Renaissance [:39]		

TABLE OF CONTENTS

CREDITS

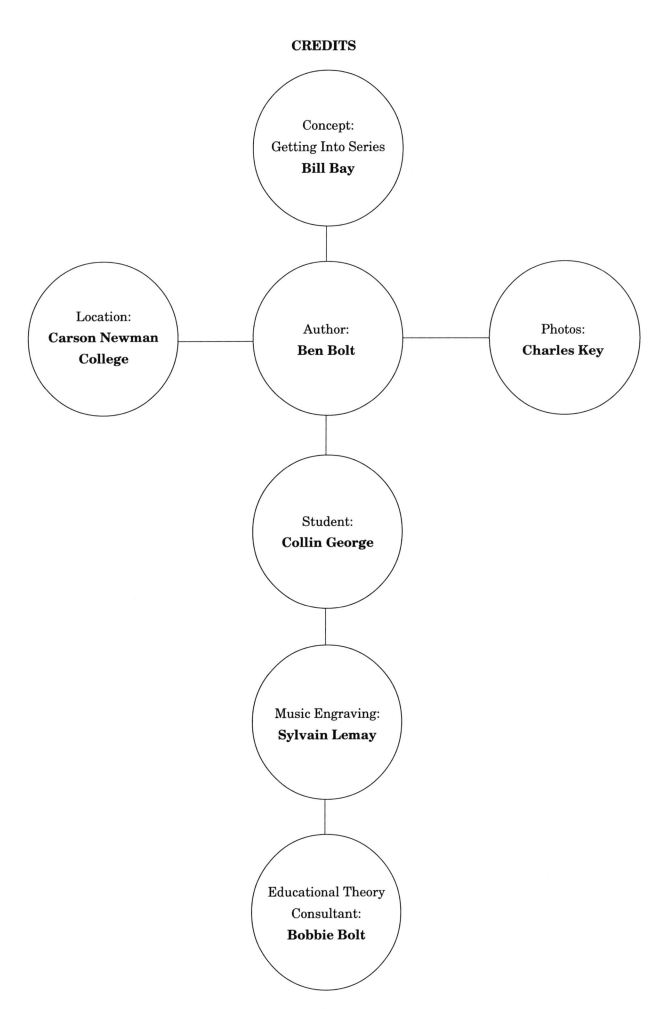

Concept:
Getting Into Series
Bill Bay

Location:
Carson Newman College

Author:
Ben Bolt

Photos:
Charles Key

Student:
Collin George

Music Engraving:
Sylvain Lemay

Educational Theory Consultant:
Bobbie Bolt

THE CLASSIC GUITAR
The Legenday Ignacio Fleta e Hijos

This guitar was hand built for Ben Bolt in 1976 by Fleta and Sons six months before Maestro Ignacio Fleta died in Barcelona, Spain. He was 77 years old.

INTRODUCTION

Hello, my name is Ben Bolt. I hope you will have as much fun as I did getting into classic guitar. It's really not hard at all, provided you learn the fundamentals. However, it is time consuming. I don't know any great guitarist who regretted the time it took to learn. In fact, if you ask a concert guitarist about their schooling days, you'll most certainly hear them chuckle and smile.

This manual is mostly for people who already play guitar a little and want to get into classic guitar. Or possibly, they know some classical techniques and want to have a more in depth understanding of cause and effect. My goal is to get you started and stay engaged with the most beautiful instrument in the world, your guitar.

The topics covered are outlined on the Table of Contents page. Ask yourself: how much time will I need to complete each task? It will depend entirely on your circumstances. Knowing what type of student you are, getting a guitar that inspires you, and most importantly, receiving encouragement from the people with whom you associate will determine your level of success.

The scope of your desire resembles the pieces of a puzzle. It's not enough to understand each piece of the puzzle intellectually. You must synthesize the information with your hands physically on the instrument, experimenting and trying new ideas. In other words, you must practice.

"If you always do what you've always done,
you'll always get what you've always gotten."

Ben Bolt

NOTATION / TABLATURE CHART

tabla sinóptica de los equísonos

"Searching for the answers to your questions is like finding hidden treasure. The gold belongs to those who dive right in, and dig!" — Ben Bolt

This chart is the best! Why? Because it tells you the name of the note, what it looks like, and everywhere it can be played on the (fretboard). The secret to great sight-reading stands boldly in front of you! Can't see it yet? Keep looking you'll find it!

TUNING

I can teach anyone how to tune a guitar. But that doesn't mean they will be in tune, including the person who just taught you how to do it! There are so many variables that one must compromise. It's the nature of the instrument, how the ear perceives sound, and weather changes, including barometric pressure fluctuations.

I will explain different ways to tune in order to give you more tricks up your sleeve, to give the illusion that you are in tune. The best cheat for this illusion is vibrato. Vibrato is a wavering of the note that goes below and above the correct pitch quickly enough that the ear perceives that you are in tune. Vibrato is an advanced technique that takes many years to master, but is well worth the effort. It's what gives the guitar its singing quality, its voice. Singing is best when treated like an instrument and an instrument, is best when treated like a voice.

I first learned how to tune with a pitch pipe. The pitch pipe is made out of six pipes representing the six strings of the guitar. It is like a miniature pipe organ. You blow into one of the pipes like you would a harmonica to get the pitch of the string. The problem with the pitch pipe is that it very quickly becomes defective one pipe at a time, because there is no way to clean it or dry it out. Oxidation from your breath affects the pitch of the note to which you are trying to tune.

A second possibility is tuning to the keyboard. The high E string is tuned to the first E above middle C (two white keys). See the diagram below.

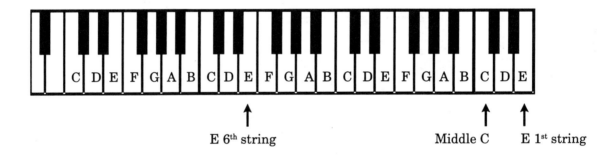

The low sixth string E is tuned to the 12th white key from the far left of the keyboard. The only time I tune like this is when I am going to play a duet with keyboard and guitar. For classic guitarists the harpsichord is the instrument of choice because it doesn't overshadow the volume of the guitar like the piano does.

A third way to tune is one I learned in Spain. A tuning fork is used. The most common tuning fork in Europe used for this purpose produces an A note. Stamped on the tuning fork I used was the number 440, which represents 440 vibrations per second. So anything that vibrates 440 vibrations per second makes the A note.

This would be the note that you hear from the first violinist or oboist for the other orchestral members to tune to as a reference before a performance. For the guitar you hold the tuning fork and strike it on your knee. Then put it up to your ear to hear the A note. This corresponds to the note on your first string at the 5th fret. Once that note is achieved you can tune the other strings, using the first string open as a reference point. I find this method very impractical, for obvious reasons. First, you must strike the tuning fork and hold it quickly to your ear. At the same time, with your other hand, you have to press the 5th fret, while simultaneously finding a finger on the same hand to play the note while you're pressing. This leaves no hand with which to tune the string unless you immediately put the tuning fork down, which means you no longer can hear the note that you are trying to tune to. So if you choose to tune this way, please use a tuning fork in E. It's the only way to go because you can sound the tuning fork with one hand and tune an open string E with the other hand. It is simple and clean.

The next way to tune, which is a common one for beginners, is estimating the pitch of the 6th string from a reference tone of a pitch pipe, a piano, or another guitar. Once this has been established, press on the 6th string at the 5th fret, which gives an A note, and that becomes your reference for the 5th string open, which happens to be an A note. You complete the process on all of the strings with one exception. To get the pitch of the 2nd string, press the 4th fret on the 3rd string, instead of the 5th. There are problems with this method. The biggest one is that the 1st string and the 6th string should sound the same, just two octaves apart. If it is off even a quarter of a tone your guitar will sound very out of tune. I do not know any professional guitarist who chooses to tune this way.

The best way for beginners that I have seen work for my students is the battery powered electronic tuner. It is inexpensive, digital, accurate, and long lasting. Only one caution: too often I notice people trying to hear with their eyes. The battery powered tuner works from a reference needle, similar to a compass. You turn the dial to the note you want to tune to, you play it on your guitar, you watch the needle move, and if it goes to the 12 o'clock position, you are in tune. The one o'clock position means the note is too high and needs to be lowered. The eleven o'clock position indicates the note is too low and needs to be raised. Newer tuners use LED lights. As long as you use it as a tool to teach your ear to hear the accurate note, I'm all for this method. The best way to accomplish this is to get a home tone, like the 6th string, in tune, and then try to tune the adjacent string without the tuner by using your ear. Then check your work with the needle to see how close you have come. In my opinion, the reason this tuning skill needs to be developed using your own ear is so that when you are performing and your guitar goes out of tune, which it often will under hot lights, you will be competent to tune on the spot. This is done after playing a chord or an open string when you have enough time to quickly reach a tuning knob to raise or lower a string. This is done in flight! It looks impressive and your audience will appreciate it.

A sixth way to tune is by harmonics. The harmonic is found on equal divisions of any stringed instrument. The example on the guitar is at the 12th fret the guitar string is divided in half. At the 7th and 19th frets the guitar string is divided into thirds. And at the 5th fret (or imaginary 24th fret), the string is divided into four equal parts. To play harmonics do not press down on the string. Instead, touch the string directly above the fret without pressing. Play and then lift your left hand finger all in one motion. Touch, play, lift. If the bell like tone is not produced, you were either not directly above the fret or the finger was lifted before you played. Remember touch, play, lift in that order. So, play a harmonic on the 6th string, 7th fret, and while it is ringing out, play the 12th fret on the 2nd string. Tune the second string to sound like the 6th. They are both B notes. Then play the 6th string 5th fret and match it to the 5th string, seventh fret, these are both E notes. These are both E notes. Next continue by playing the 5th fret, 5th string and the 7th fret, 4th string to tune the 4th string. These are A notes. Finally, play the 5th fret, 4th string and the 7th fret, 3rd string and match those tones, which are D notes. (Page 86)

This is one of my favorite ways to tune because there is no string interruption, meaning pressing down. Both notes ring out and you are able to hear both notes clearly in tune because of the characteristic long duration of the harmonic tone. I tuned this way for ten years. But this method has problems as well. The biggest one is that a harmonic represents a perfect world, the perfect division of a string into equal parts, meaning omitting frets to get the note because you do not press down. However, the guitar is not a particularly perfect world, especially with the matter of tuning. The variables include pressing on the string too hard, bending the string too much, and various weather conditions. Consequently, if you tune to a perfect world but music is made imperfectly merely from the act of pressing down on the strings, you will always have to be making adjustments as you play.

The best option that I have found for me personally is a technique which tunes from the outside strings inward using only the open strings. I find this to be more accurate.

Step One: Get the 1st string in tune.
Step Two: Play the 1st string and 6th string, back and forth or at the same time. Make sure the E strings sound the same. The 6th string is two octaves lower.
Step Three: Play the 6th string and 2nd string, back and forth or at the same time. Tune to an interval of a perfect fifth, E to B.
Step Four: Play the 1st string and 5th string, back and forth or at the same time. Tune to an interval of a perfect fifth, A to E.
Step Five: Play the 5th string and the 4th string, back and forth or at the same time. Tune to an interval of a perfect fourth, A to D.
Step Six: Play the 4th string and the 3rd string, back and forth or at the same time. Tune to an interval of a perfect fourth, D to G.

These are all easy intervals to train your ear to hear. The first note, the fourth note, and the fifth note of any scale are the most important. If you are in the key of E, this would be E notes, A notes, and B notes, which happen to be open strings. In the key of A, this would be A notes, D notes, and E notes, which also happen to be open strings. And finally, in the key of D, this would be D notes, G notes, and A notes, which are also open strings. These are all very common keys in which we play on the classic guitar.

CHANGING STRINGS

When to Change Strings

Sometimes it's obvious when to change strings. Examples would be a broken string, the winding of one of the bass strings unraveling, or a false string. A false string is not true to the octave. To tell if it is, you would play the harmonic at the 12th fret on the string. Listen and then press down at the 12th fret without the harmonic. They should sound identical. This is called a unison. It's possible to have a true string in the beginning and it becomes untrue (false). The best example of that would be when a steel string or an electric string has too much rust, which interrupts the vibration.

Other times to change strings become more obvious with experience. Examples would be when bass strings start sounding so mellow that they become muddy. Or the treble strings may sound like plastic. Even though treble strings are made out of a plastic polymer, they should not sound like plastic. The metaphor I often use with students is this: If the fish smells fishy, don't eat it.

And last, but not least, you will change them based upon your knowledge of how long you can play on them until they peak. You want them to peak for a live performance, for example. Let's say you practice two hours a day and your strings typically peak in three weeks. You would want to change them about three weeks before the performance. Exceptions would be if you had two guitars, one that you did the bulk of your practicing on, and one you used for performances. You would adjust accordingly.

HOW TO CHANGE STRINGS

Because classic guitar strings do not have a ball end, like electric and acoustic guitar strings, they must be tied. There are many misconceptions about how to tie a classic guitar string.

Misconception

#1: Have as much of the string wound around the tuning roller as possible, beginning with the very end of the string.

#2: Make the string look as beautiful as possible around the tuning roller.

#3: You only need to go over and under two times before tightening the string.

#4: Your guitar is not staying in tune and you suspect you have a bad set of strings, which does happen occasionally.

The Truth

#1: It's not how many times the string is wrapped around the roller that keeps it from slipping. It's how it's tied.

#2: The more times the string crosses over itself in an unpredictable sort of way, it creates more of a clamping effect that prevents slippage, much like the grooves of a screw versus the smoothness of a nail shaft.

#3: I tie over and under four times with the exception of the sixth string, where I go over and under three times, due to the increased thickness of that string. This virtually eliminates slipping, but doesn't eliminate stretching.

#4: A string can only go out of tune two ways. It is either slipping or stretching. Regardless of the string manufacturer or how you tie them, it is normal for all strings to stretch over a short period of time. A string slipping can go on indefinitely until it finally breaks.

HOW TO CHANGE STRINGS

Step 1: Slip the string through the hole in the bridge first from the sound hole side. This is to avoid unnecessary damage to the string lining for bass strings or scratching for treble strings.

Step 2: Take the short end of the string and go away from yourself and under the long side of the string to form a loop.

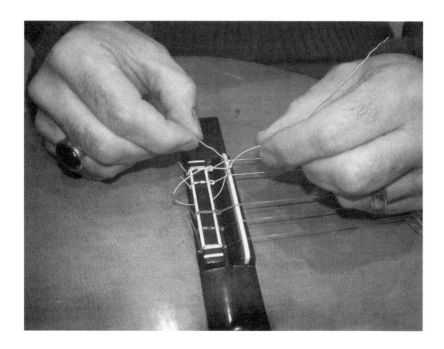

Step 3: Go over and under one time.

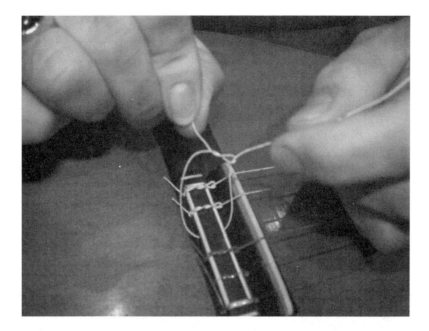

While holding the short end, continue this process two or three more times, depending on how thick the string is. Notice how tightly I am holding onto the short end of the string.

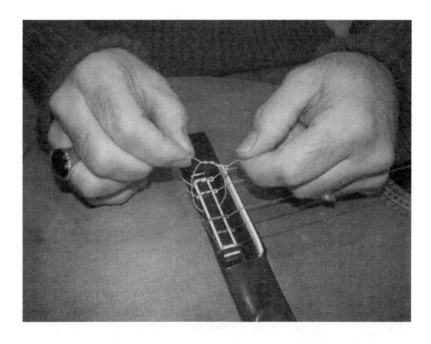

Step 4: Jockey your hands back and forth, similarly to flossing your teeth, until the string is tight against the tie block of the bridge. Be careful and go easy because it is easy to scratch the lining of the bass strings. The treble strings should not be a problem in this regard.

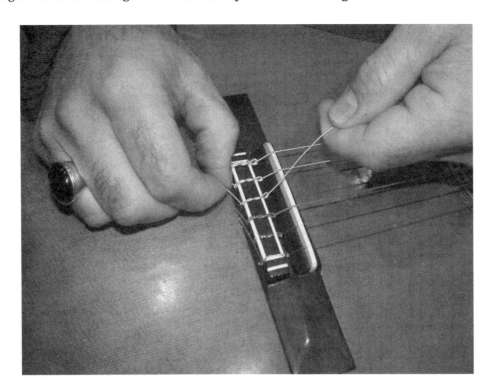

Notice in the next picture that the short end and the long end of the string meet together on the back side of the tie block. If you don't do this with the treble strings, they can slip out and make an ugly mark on your beautiful guitar.

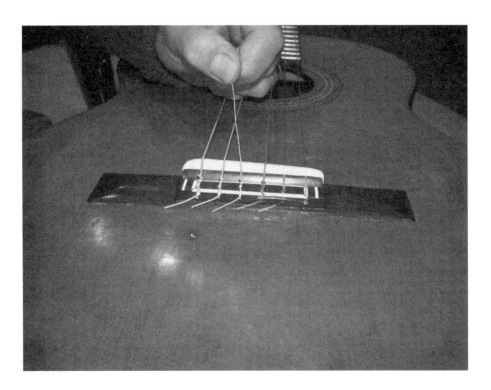

Step 5: Pull the string through the peg roller in the headstock while holding the string.

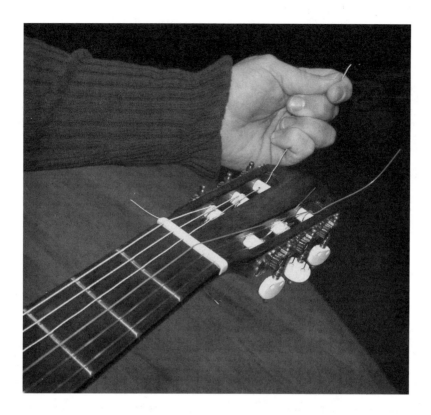

Step 6: Pull the short end of the string toward your body.

Step 7: Wind the short end of the string under and over four times while still holding on to the short end.

Step 8: While still holding onto the short end of the string, pull it straight up, in line with the rest of the string. You should hear a little click sound.

Step 9: As you are holding on to the short end of the string, start tightening it around the string roller.

Here is what your strings will look like on the headstock when you are finished tying.

WHAT KIND OF LEARNER ARE YOU?

It is important for you to understand how your brain processes information, particularly when it is information that you want for your own personal enjoyment, in this case, playing the guitar.

Pictured below are educationally accepted styles of learning. Each of us possesses the ability to learn from all of our senses. When learning music the senses of smell and taste are not particularly useful. However, learning by seeing, hearing, touching, and sensing are all important. Everyone has preferred senses that work best for them. We are not all wired the same.

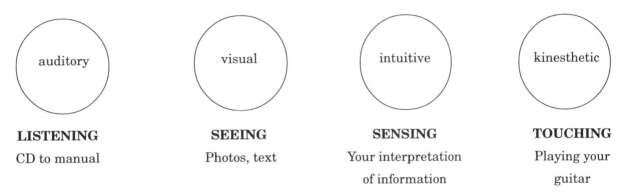

When you are in your car listening to the CD that accompanies this manual, you are using 100% of your auditory learning ability.

When you study the photographs or read the text, as well as the music, you are a totally visual learner.

When you pick up your guitar and play with your eyes closed and ears covered, exploring what it feels like to touch your instrument, you are using your sense of touch, which is known as kinesthetic learning.

When you take off the earmuffs and open your eyes, you will find yourself using a combination of auditory, visual, and kinesthetic! During the playing of a piece of music, the percentage of use of all three of these styles of learning changes constantly. An example: you started out studying electric guitar with dots on the fingerboard. Now you have a classic guitar with no dots and you have to make a jump from the first position to the eighth position and you keep missing it (and you also miss your dots). In that moment, 100% visual learning takes over.

When I see a guitar player whose intuition is in tune with the truth of good guitar playing, who respects a straight line, for instance, most people simply call it natural ability. However, those who only have natural ability never seem to last very long with this instrument. My opinion is that everyone needs a challenge in order to stay interested, something that keeps you coming back for more. This is why a great guitar player will never say they have it all figured out. They still take their boxing lessons, like everyone else.

We are all intuitive, some more than others. Basically, if you think you can or you think you can't, you're right. Intuition is knowing without experiencing, a futuristic prediction of yourself. To develop your intuition takes only one thing: to know it exists.

BEFORE COLLIN'S FIRST CLASSIC GUITAR LESSON WITH BEN BOLT

BAD HABITS?

How can he not notice the muffled first and second strings? I see more good players losing because of that left hand thumb hung over the neck. I'll fix that real quick when he stops... if he'll let me.

"There is no such thing as bad habits; therefore, bad habits never need to be broken. The problem is that players employ correct techniques at the wrong time."

Ben Bolt

Unbelievable! Did he just read my mind? The kid's got intuition!

"Truth is guitar's middle name.
All inspired moments are sheathed in it."

Ben Bolt

I point out that in order to use the left-hand thumb as a point of reference, it must be positioned in the lower third of the guitar neck. In this way, without displacing the thumb, Collin can reach for bass strings without accidentally muting the treble strings.

"One note skillfully played can light a concert hall."

Ben Bolt

There should also be a space between the bottom of the guitar neck and the left-hand palm. Actually, the student's palm could be closer than I am showing. Using a pencil instead of my little finger would be an even better example for this illustration. However, this approach gives me a chance to learn about the lad's personality. This is the first body contact ten minutes into his first lesson.

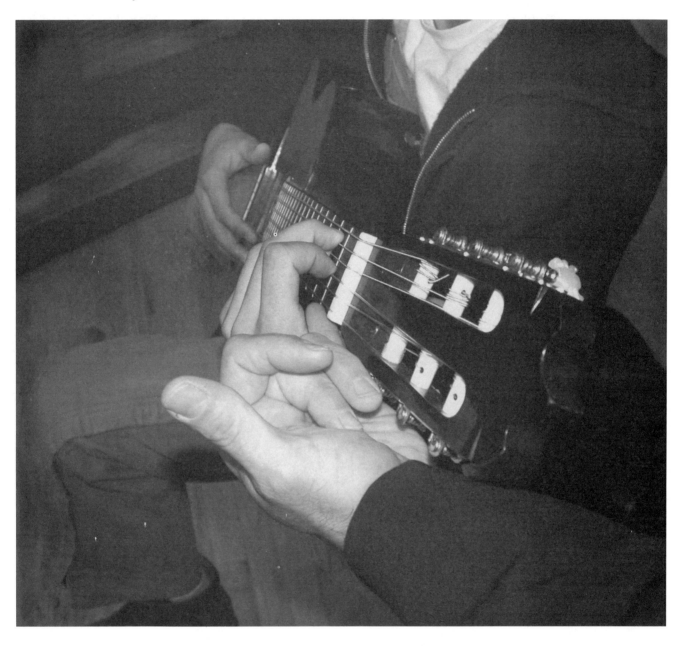

"Sometimes it's what you don't do that makes a difference.
Don't touch the neck with the palm of your hand in the classic style."

Ben Bolt

Because of the limits of a thirty minute lesson, I immediately switch to the right hand. Collin is given my guide for a good right-hand position, as I emphasize that this is in general. Like verbs, there are exceptions. The guide is that all fingers, including the thumb, are placed on the third string. This prevents the thumb and the fingers from colliding during flight, since they follow through in opposite directions.

Now go get your guitar and try it. It's easy and it works!

"In guitar technique, you only have to respect one thing: the straight line.
Therefore, there's only one rule: the string is the boss."

Ben Bolt

This is the first time I show him so that he can see my hand. I'm careful not to play anything. This would be a basic hand position if the 6th string was about to be played and the other fingers were playing some treble strings, like an E Minor arpeggio.

"Sound reasons are the foundation of all music.
The heart of music has its own reasons, which reason will never know."

Ben Bolt

After twenty minutes he trusts me. I don't correct his left-hand thumb. I let him sit the way he wants. And it looks like we have known each other for years. Just twenty minutes... what luck I had. He didn't even know he was going to have his picture taken and neither did I! We spent the rest of the time talking guitar. He comments on the beautiful hall and I tell him that the Los Angeles Guitar Quartet like it too. "You're kidding, when were they here? I can't believe it, they're my favorite!"

The perfect lesson. He never asked me why a camera was there for his first lesson, I'm not sure he even noticed.

"In the end, it's the music that's left standing."
Ben Bolt

MODELS OF LEARNING

The Truest Test of Anything is Time.

Two models of learning are pictured below. The one on the right represents the traditional model of learning where a teacher instructs and a student receives the information. Some people call this the "Open the mouth and pour the knowledge down the throat" model.

The second model, on the left, illustrates a higher level of learning, where one takes what has been learned and uses it to produce new information. For a guitarist, this could be a new interpretation of how to play a piece, or it could be a whole new composition, or anything else that allowed you, the guitarist, to take the knowledge you had received, and to use it to produce something original for you.

Too often education culminates with the receiving of knowledge. Nothing original happens beyond that. Try to allow yourself to trust your intuition to experiment and create with the knowledge you are gaining.

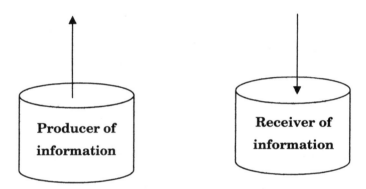

At the time I was learning to play the classic guitar, I was lucky to have a teacher who encouraged me to understand the logic behind what I was learning. I was discouraged from blindly memorizing concepts and allowing dogma to dominate my opinions. "Personally speaking, the best teachers allow students to challenge all information as long as they remain sincere and really do want to learn. With such a partnership between student and teacher, the trajectory of the guitar will always be vertical and ascending!"

Ben Bolt

THE "DUTCH UNCLE"

"My way or the highway!"

What's he doing? He's turned the delicate instrument into a club. Strict and stubborn, he will not bend the rules of the game. It's wise for the student to not even suggest a change with the program. Believe it or not, this kind of teacher can help you. He can be a nice guy if he sees you're sincere. When all else fails, follow directions. He's the one that will do exactly that.

THE "BRAGGER"

"I did more for the guitar..."

Who's he trying to kid? Even a beginner can smell a phony. Everything this teacher says should be subject to suspicion and checked out. Remember this: the guitar doesn't have any debts. It doesn't owe you or me a dime. We owe it, period!

THE "PROUD" TEACHER

"Loyalty means everything to me."

He puts the guitar first and can be flexible. This teacher is a little closer to the European School of Thought. He's on your side 100%. One warning: If you decide to study with someone else, be certain of your decision. It could be difficult to get him back on your side again if it doesn't work out with your new teacher.

THE "PROFOUND" PROFESSOR

**"Notes written on a piece of paper can never be music.
They are merely a roadmap to a destination called music."**

Good luck finding this one. He's rare, unflappable, never forces, is knowledgeable, friendly, kind, and credible. He's more than happy to take you back if you leave him for another teacher and he'll do it without hesitation. This one can calm your parents down once you've announced you want to become a professional guitarist. It's just a question of time before destiny puts him in a bigger fishpond. Learn all you can, while you can.

SITTING POSITION

Step 1: Sit on the front edge of the chair. Place the guitar on your left leg. The guitar only touches the left leg. You will need to steady the guitar with your left hand.

Two Points of Contact

Step 2: Bring your right leg around and touch the guitar at the same time that your right forearm holds the guitar down on both legs. This is done simultaneously, like a wave: right leg, right forearm. Only the weight of the right forearm is used. There is no need to push down.

Three Points of Contact

Step 3: Move forward from the waist, keeping your spinal chord straight until you touch the top left portion of the back of the guitar.

Four Points of Contact

Notice my stomach is not touching the guitar. If it did, it would seriously affect the resonance of the guitar. Of course, it will if I don't get on that diet again!

Step 4: Place the fingers of the right hand on the strings to be played first. This is called right-hand preparation.

Five Points of Contact

Step 5: Present your left hand to the fingerboard,

Six Points of Contact

Step 6: Let the music begin!

FREE STROKE
Preparation of the Index Finger

Notice the joint closest to the tip of the finger does not collapse.

REST STROKE
Follow Through of the Index Finger

The joint closest to the tip of the finger collapses during follow through.

I file my nails with a Revlon shaping and finishing metal flake file. This is not the kind of file that has ridges. Files with ridges will rip into your nail. There are two sizes, buy the smaller size. It is easier to control. After that I finish the process with 400-600 grit sand paper. Don't use the wet and dry kind. Use TRI-M-Ote Fre-cut Paper A wt. Open Coat made by 3M. The edge of the fingernail should be as smooth as glass, no roughness, no pit marks, glassy smooth when you are done.

FINGERNAILS

Fingernails will give you the most options for varying tone and dynamics. Tone refers to how metallic or mellow a sound is while dynamics indicates how loud or soft a note is. In classic guitar, styles of music range from Baroque and Renaissance to Spanish and avant-garde, to name a few.

I have personally found that fingernails allow my students to explore their interpretive ideas to the maximum. We only use fingernails on the right hand and through curving the finger and engaging only fingernail creates a metallic tone. This is good for crisp, clean, bright, light tones that can mimic flutes, triangle, or even an oboe. Remember what Ludwig Von Beethoven said after hearing the guitar for the first time? "It's a miniature orchestra within itself." If you engage a combination of fingernail and flesh the tone becomes sweeter, which can imitate the flute, the clarinet, or even the cello.

Technically speaking, it's easier and a lot more accurate to play with fingernails. I don't know of any world class concert guitar player who plays without using fingernails. Everyone can't be wrong!

May I throw a wrench in the works? Growing, maintaining, and using fingernails can be extremely frustrating. If you break a fingernail before a concert, it is equivalent to having a guitarist using a flatpick being handed a jagged rough partial piece of a pick to use for that performance. Any guitarist using a flatpick in that situation would simply reach in his pocket and grab another pick. I envy them. We classic guitarists have to put our audience on hold for at least two weeks to a month...(just kidding). We do have ridiculous options: Play without the fingernail, use Crazy Glue to mend it, which can be frightening backstage. For example, you could glue your fingernails (and I'm not kidding). Or you could put on an artificial nail. It represents a perfect world. You simply glue it on and it plays like steel. If you break one, you can quickly grab another one and glue it on. I used them for three straight years until I developed a very serious fungal infection...that I still have at this writing after having spent more than $1000 on anti-fungal medications. So from personal experience, I hesitate to recommend the use of artificial nails. However, in emergencies, you have no other choice.

If you have weak fingernails, and most guitarists do in the beginning, be assured they do get stronger with use as the attack and release of the string from the nail promotes blood circulation. The only way to have healthy nails is to approach the problem nutritionally. I use Biotin for my fingernails and it has helped. It's available at health food stores. Some of you may have heard that gelatin helps, but it's made from animal hooves, mostly horses. Two of my best friends are horses, my horses. So I wasn't impressed with consuming my friends' feet. However, they do have intermittent hoof problems, just like people can have nail problems, fungal infections, etc. Veterinarians recommend Biotin for strengthening horses' hooves. It's just a vitamin, folks. So I started snitching my horses' vitamins. Later I found out research has been done in England which proves it also works for people who want stronger nails or healthier skin. Out of curiosity, I checked at my local health food store and discovered it is readily available on the shelf.

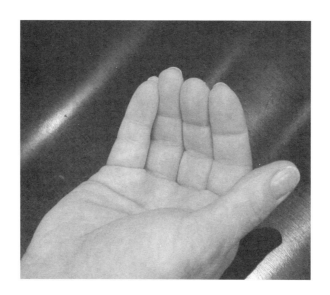

STRING ATTACK

 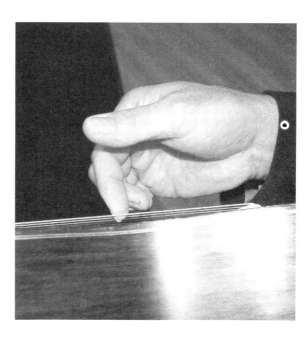

For the fullest sound, a combination of nail and flesh touches the string in preparation of the string attack. The position of my hand in both photographs is incorrect. As a matter of fact, if you need to see your right-hand fingers playing the strings, it will throw your right-hand position off. There are only six strings; therefore, the right hand learns very quickly how to judge where the strings are located.

FUNGI IS NO FUN

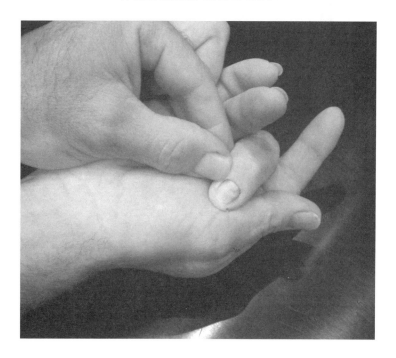

In the previous photo, on page 39 (top) the middle fingernail cannot be seen. This is because of fungus reeking havoc with the natural growing process. The darkened area around the cuticle is a blue-green color. Gardening, working in the food preparation business, or in my case, using artificial fingernails, can cause this painful infection. If you think you might have this problem, please see your doctor ASAP. The only way to get rid of it is to take anti-fungal drugs. Don't put it off!

BEVELING YOUR FINGERNAILS

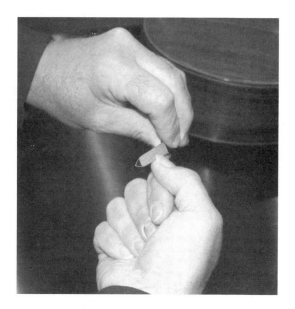

Over many years of trial and error, my research has revealed this: beveling the fingernail gives the best sound, with faster release from the string, as well as helping the fingers glide smoothly across the strings without the fingernail catching. Notice the angle at which the file is held during the shaping process.

THE RIGHT HAND

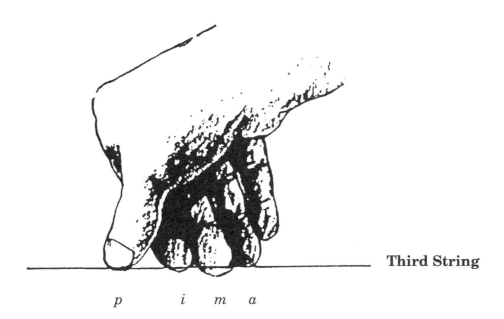

Third String

p i m a

STROKES

The rest stroke using the thumb: Place a on the first string, m on the second string, and i on the third string. Play the sixth string slowly. As you glide over the string, follow through until you reach the fifth string. You should end up resting on string number 5. Practice on all bass strings (6, 5, and 4).

The rest stroke using the fingers: Place the thumb (p) on the sixth string. Play the third string slowly with your index (i) finger. As your finger glides slowly over the string, follow through until you rest on string number 4. Practice using your middle finger (m) on the second string and your ring finger (a) on the first string. Also, practice alternating $i\ m$, $i\ a$, and $m\ a$ on the treble strings (1, 2, and 3). I use i and a because they are similar in length on my hand. You should collapse the joint closest to the tip of the finger during the follow-through.

Free stroke: In using free stroke, the finger does not rest. The joint closest to the tip of the finger does not collapse. You must be careful not to get under the string and pull up with the finger. As an experiment, you can try pulling the string straight up and releasing it. This will cause a slap against the fingerboard and should be avoided. However, rock bass players use this technique as an effect that sounds good!

Regardless of which stroke is used, the flesh and fingernail should touch the string at the same time when you're preparing to play. This technique produces the best tone.

CHORDS
Preparation of the Right Hand

Fingers are webbed together, thumb is separate from fingers.

Chord Preparation with Correct Sitting Position

I am keeping the joint closest to the tip of my fingers straight as an option to obtain more volume.

Chords – Right Hand Preparation from Performer's Point of View

Preparation of a Three Note Chord Using *p, m, a*

Notice the thumb will play with flesh only. The fingernail is not presented to the string. This is an option for tone color in the bass line.

MUSIC THEORY

Pitch

Music is written on five lines. These lines are called the **staff**. The notes can be written on the lines or in the spaces between the lines.

Notes above or below the staff require additional lines as a continuation of the staff. These lines are called **ledger lines**.

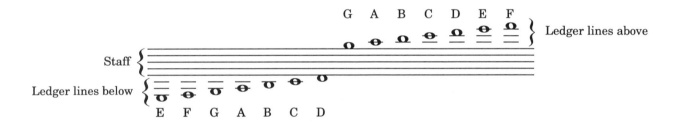

The musical alphabet uses the first seven letters of the language alphabet: A, B, C, D, E, F, G. After G, the next letter is A again. From any letter to the same letter is called an octave. There are eight letters in an octave.

One octave: C D E F G A B C

At the beginning of every staff, you will notice a sign called the **clef sign**. In guitar music, we use the G or treble clef sign.

Clef Sign

Sharps, Flats, and Naturals

Sharps, flats, and naturals raise or lower a note by 1 fret. A 1-fret distance on the guitar is called a **half step** in music (or **half tone**). Each sharp, flat, and natural has a sign that is placed before the note.

Sharp   ♯   raises the note by 1 fret.

Flat   ♭   lowers the note by 1 fret.

Natural   ♮   restores the note to its regular pitch after it was raised or lowered.

Once a note is altered, it remains altered for the entire measure.

The way a note is written determines the length of the note's duration

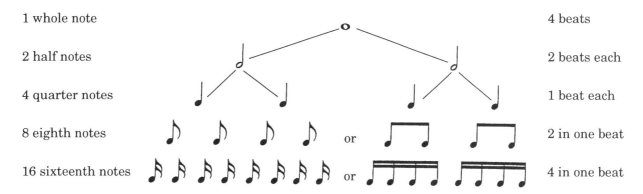

1 whole note	4 beats
2 half notes	2 beats each
4 quarter notes	1 beat each
8 eighth notes	2 in one beat
16 sixteenth notes	4 in one beat

Rests

For every note value there is a corresponding rest having the same time value.

Whole   Half   Quarter   Eighth   Sixteenth

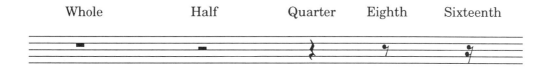

Music is arithmetically divided into **measures** by vertical bars in the staff. The number of beats in each measure is determined by the time signature placed after the clef.

$$\frac{2}{4} \qquad \frac{3}{4} \qquad \frac{4}{4} \qquad \frac{3}{8} \qquad \frac{6}{8} \quad \text{etc.}$$

The top number tells how many beats in a measure, while the bottom number tells what kind of note receives one beat.

3	=	3 beats to the measure
4	=	1 quarter note per beat
		or the equivalent:
		2 eighth notes per beat
		or 4 sixteenth notes per beat, etc.

The most common time signature is $\frac{4}{4}$. It is also marked **C**.

Key Signature

When the tonality requires that certain notes are to be sharp or flat throughout a composition, the sharps or flats are grouped together at the beginning of each staff, forming the key signature. This affects every note of the same name throughout the musical piece.

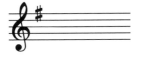   All F notes are to be played F sharp.

The Dot

A dot placed to the right of a note lengthens it by one half:

These dots can also be placed to the right of rests:

$$\xi\cdot \; = \; \gamma \quad \gamma \quad \gamma$$

The Double Sharp

A double sharp placed before a note raises it by 2 frets, or a whole tone. G double sharp will sound like A.

The sign looks like this: ✖

The Double Flat

A double flat lowers a note 2 frets, or a whole tone. E double flat will sound like D.

The sign uses two flats before a note: ♭♭

Repeats

Repeat the preceding.

Repeat the following.

Repeat the preceding and repeat the following.

The Tie

When a note is tied to the same note, the first note rings out the duration of both notes. Don't play the second note.

Slurs

When a note is tied to a different note; you play the first note with your right hand and make the second note sound with your left hand. Slurs are also called hammer-ons or pull-offs.

THE RIGHT HAND
Fingering

English	Symbol	Spanish
thumb	*p*	pulgar
index	*i*	indice
middle	*m*	medio
ring	*a*	anular

Position

The best way to learn a good right-hand position is to place *i, m,* and *a* on third string. Place your thumb on the third string as well, keeping the thumb to the left of the index finger. (page 25)

ARPEGGIOS USING OPEN STRINGS

(the bass line should sound the loudest)

Track
#1

* Not all examples in
this excercise are
included on recording.

p = thumb
i = index
m = middle
a = ring

Ben Bolt

48

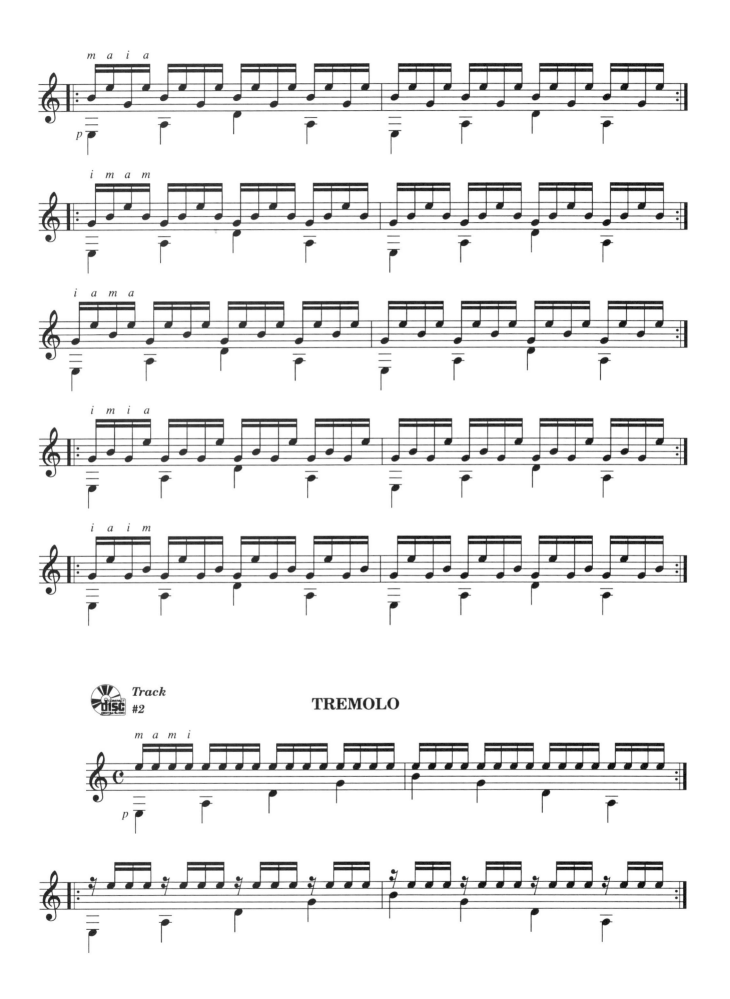

TREMOLO

RIGHT HAND STUDIES

Ben Bolt

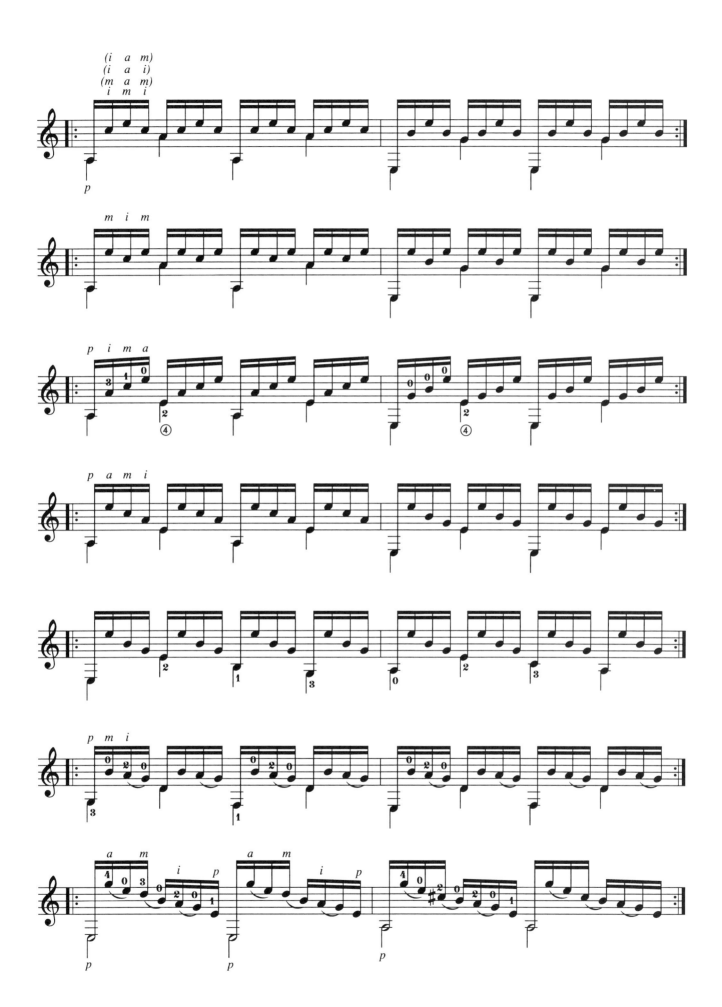

THE LEFT HAND

Fingering

index	=	1
middle	=	2
ring	=	3
little finger	=	4

Position

Because music changes pitch and direction, the left hand also needs to follow that motion. This makes explaining the left-hand position difficult, because it depends on your technical needs at that time. However, there are some practical and general concepts to keep in mind.

First, the fingernails of the left hand should be short enough so that they do not touch the fingerboard of the guitar. Second, the thumb should be placed generally in the middle of the back of the neck between the index and middle fingers. (See sketch.)

Third, the fingers should always be placed directly behind the frets. This gives the best tone and helps to teach your arm and finger exactly where each note is. Correct muscular memory begins here. Last, when playing scale passages, the knuckles should be parallel to the fingerboard.

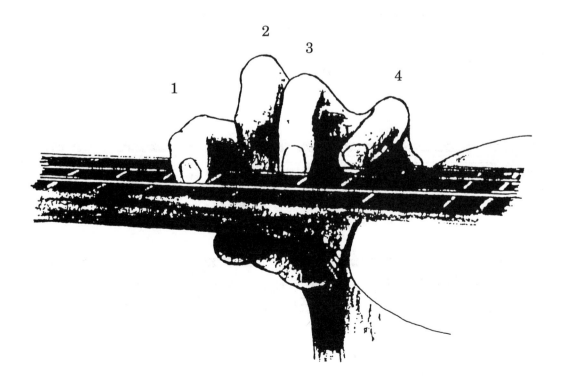

PERPENDICULAR PRESENTATION OF LEFT HAND
When two or more fingers are on the same fret

The wrist will naturally curve more, as you have the need to place more fingers on the same fret. The A chord using three fingers on the second fret would be an example of needing more angle between the hand and forearm.

CLASSIC CHORD PROGRESSION

Track #4

Ben Bolt

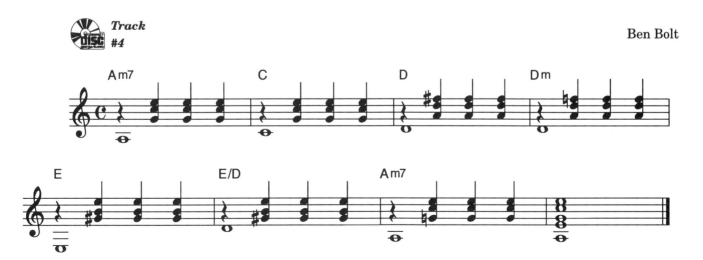

DIAGONAL PRESENTATION OF THE LEFT HAND
When fingertips form a diagonal line across the fretboard

The middle finger appearing to be over the fret is an illusion, just like in the parallel presentation. The little finger is not pressing down, although it appears to be. If it was I would most likely produce a cracked note on the third string due to the fact that the finger was not placed behind the fret. If you have difficulty separating fingers two and three enough to place them behind consecutive frets, you are not alone. The reason for this is that when your fingers are extended, there is great separation between fingers two and three. But as you present them to the fretboard, the curvature of fingers two and three create the ram's horn effect. The ram's horn is my metaphor for two fingertips coming at sharp angles toward each other when they curve.

PARALLEL PRESENTATION OF THE LEFT HAND

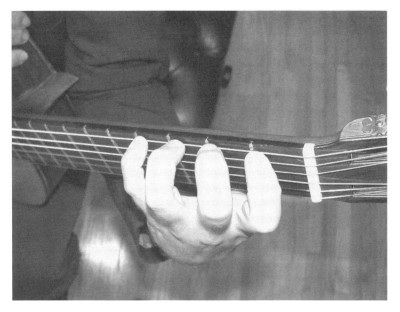

Notice my middle finger once again appears to be over the second fret. I do this to enable my ring finger to be behind the fret. This eliminates the risk of buzzing. You can really see the "Ram's horn effect" in these photos.

Parallel presentation, six string, elbow close to the body, wrist bent, fingers less curved.

6th string parallel presentation is the easiest to do. Logic dictates the wrist position because of the possibility of needing to play on the treble strings at the same time.

Parallel presentation on the first string, elbow away from the body, wrist straight, fingers curved. This presentation requires more time to perfect. As you go from the 1st to the 6th strings, the curvature of the fingers becomes less curved, the elbow heads toward your torso, and, finally, the wrist step by step becomes more and more curved. If you allowed your wrist to stay curved when you arrived at the first string, there would be no control as well, thus losing your best point of reference for your left hand, your thumb.

LEFT HAND
Incorrect Presentation of the Index Finger for the C Note, Second String, First Fret

Notice that the second and third fingers are traveling over to help the index finger do its job. Remember, it never pays to rob Peter for Paul.

Correct Presentation

Notice that the middle finger is hovering over the second fret while the index finger is pressing down. This is critical for your success as a technician on the guitar. Each finger should do its job without the help of the other fingers.

NATURAL NOTES IN THE FIRST POSITION

Track #5

Ben Bolt

POSITIONS

There are as many positions as frets. The factor that determines the position that you're in is the location of your index finger. Regardless if it is being used or not at that moment.

EXAMPLE

| position 4 | position 3 | position 2 | position 1 |

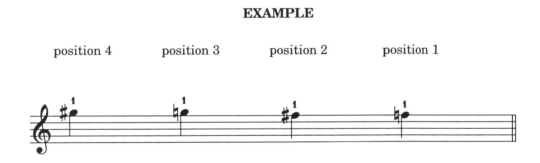

Finger 4 stays down in all four chords. It's o.k. to let your arm do most of the work transporting your hand.

| position 1 | position 2 | position 3 | position 4 |

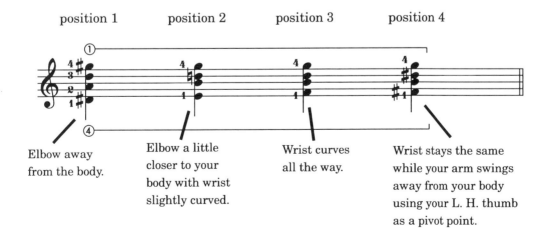

Elbow away from the body.

Elbow a little closer to your body with wrist slightly curved.

Wrist curves all the way.

Wrist stays the same while your arm swings away from your body using your L. H. thumb as a pivot point.

MILITARY STEP
Parallel Presentation of the Left Hand

Ben Bolt

Track #6

Left-Hand Fingers: 1, 2, 3, 4

Right-Hand Fingers: *i m / m i / m a / a m / i a / a i*

POINT OF REFERENCE

Track #7

P.O.R. refers to the concept of using the finger as a pivot point. While the finger is held down and the note is ringing, your arm takes the other fingers to the desired location. (↓)

Ex. 1

Ex. 2 - P.O.R. could also be written like this:

If you respect the rests in exercise two, the music will sound like it has hiccups. Start to develop your "Beginner Intuition". P.O.R. not only lets the music breathe, It will give you technical command of your instrument.

SLURS

(⌢ or ⌣)

Slurs can be either ascending or descending in nature. The first note is played by your right hand while, the second note is performed with your left hand.

ascending   descending

Make certain the second note is as loud as the first!

59

PACHELBEL'S CANON

Andante

arr. Ben Bolt

DOUBLE NOTE DANCE

To Jason Vieaux

Track #9

Ben Bolt

Allegro

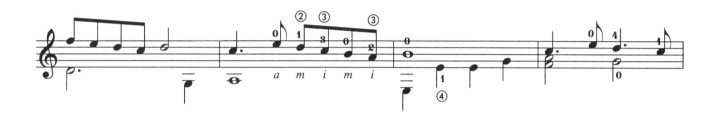

rit.

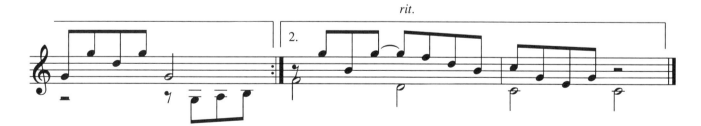

GAVOTTE

Track #10

arr. Ben Bolt   * Repeats not taken
in recording.

J.S. Bach

62

Gavotte II

* Keep your 3rd finger down.

HOUSE OF THE RISING SUN

P.O.R. = ↓

arr. Ben Bolt

left elbow close to your torso

elbow swings away from your body

DANZA LATINO
To Eduardo Fernandez

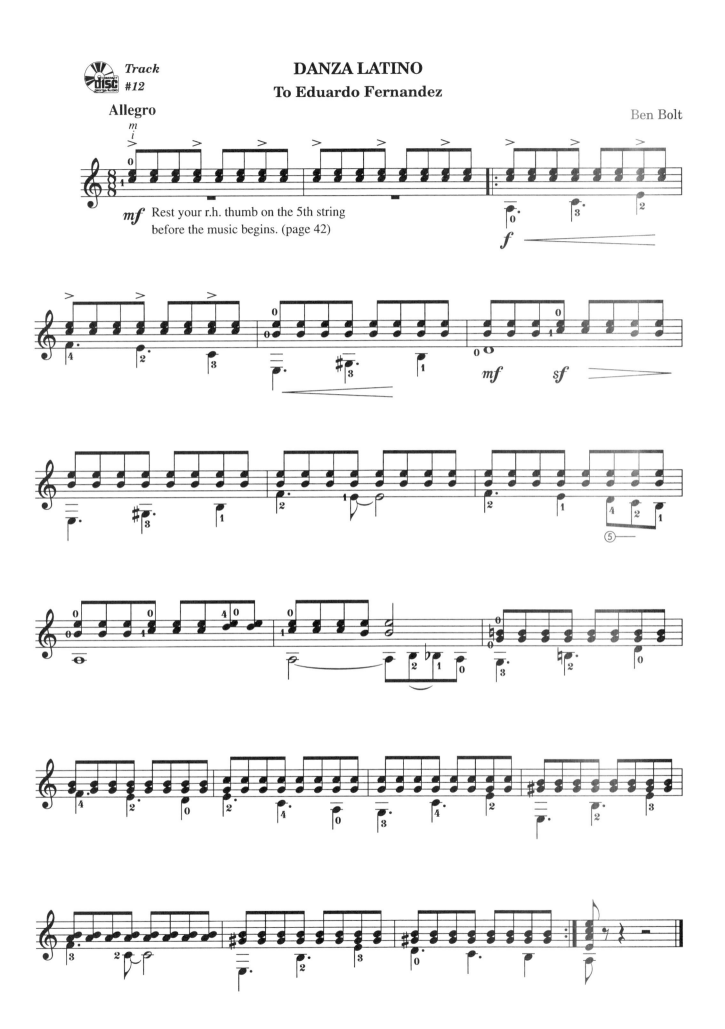

Ben Bolt

Allegro

mf Rest your r.h. thumb on the 5th string
before the music begins. (page 42)

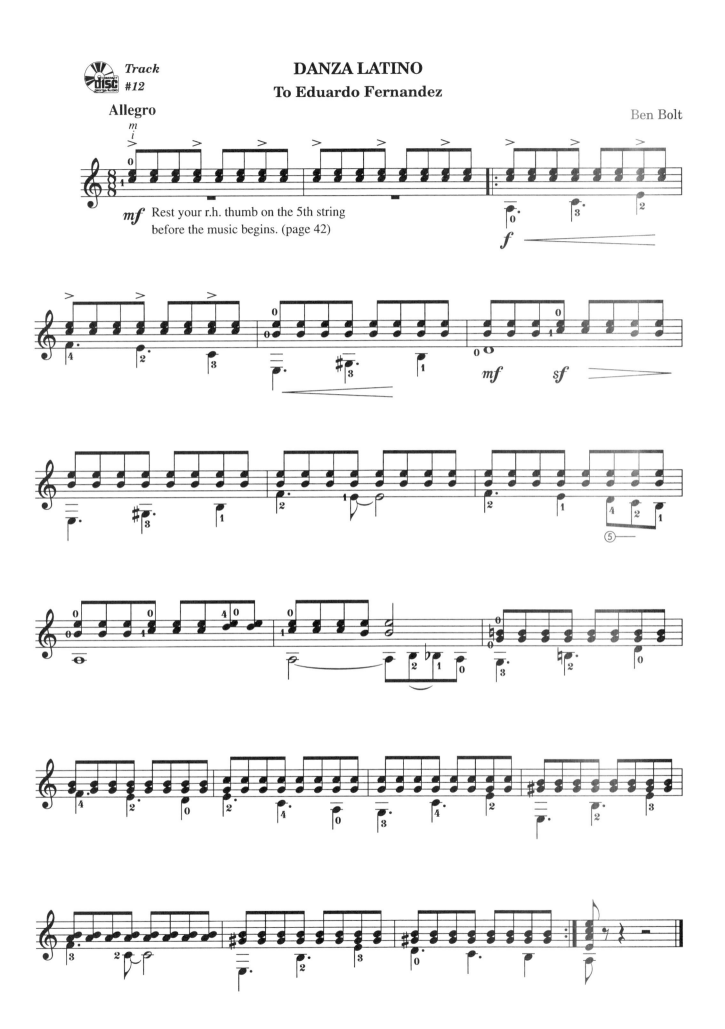

65

FÜR ELISE
(Theme)

* Repeats not taken
in recording.

Ludwig von Beethoven

arr. Ben Bolt

P.O.R.

* For training purposes, leave your l.h. second finger down during the first eight bars. (P.O.R.)
   Your l.h. arm will help carry your fingers to the correct notes.

ANITRA'S DANCE

arr. Ben Bolt

Edvard Grieg

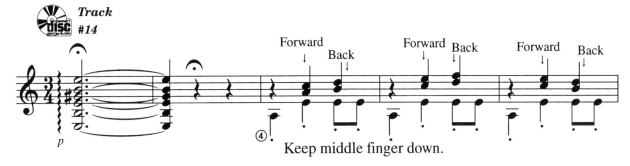

Forward Back Forward Back Forward Back

Keep middle finger down.

cresc.

* Left elbow movement.

BALBOA
Theme, Variations and Finale
To David Russell

Ben Bolt

THE ZONE

Track #15

* Repeats not taken
in recording.

Track
#16

AMADOR

Ben Bolt

Allegro

Var. 1

69

Track
#17

GAMBOA

Ben Bolt

Var. 2

SOSA HILL

Ben Bolt

Var. 3
Diablo

pizz. sempre
(mute all notes w/ the palm of your right hand)

SANTA CLARA

Var. 4
Finale

71

ANDANTE

Track #20

arr. Ben Bolt

Fernando Sor

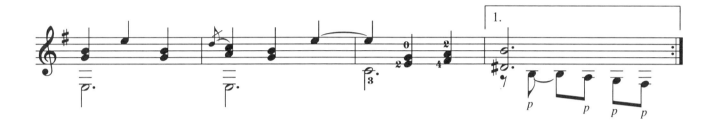

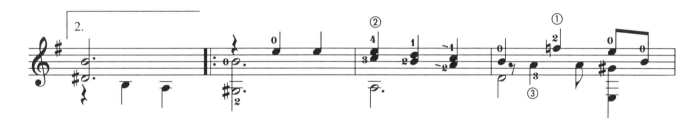

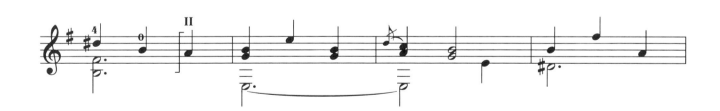

ANDANTE

arr. Ben Bolt

Fernando Sor

Track #21

---

* The double dot should last the duration of seven sixteenth notes. Why? Because a quarter note is equal to four sixteenth notes. One dot lengthens a note by half of its value. In this case add two more sixteenth notes. A dot placed after a dot lengthens the note by one half of the first dot (one sixteenth). 4+2+1=7. If you don't pay attention to this part of your music theory, a watered down sixteenth will be played, sounding more like an eighth note.

HYMN FOR ZADOK
To Rick Foster

Ben Bolt

Track #22

* On the recording, first time, you will hear me crack the B note. This happened because I sent the command from my brain to both hands, play! This means my L. H. was not quite ready for my R. H. to attack. One fraction of a second (delay) causes "the cracked note". What a down. However, I was ready on the repeat. I pressed down the L. H. finger first, then I allowed my R. H. to play. Notice even the tone improved.

"Sometimes you will learn more from my imperfection".

Ben Bolt

STREETS OF PARIS
To Andy York

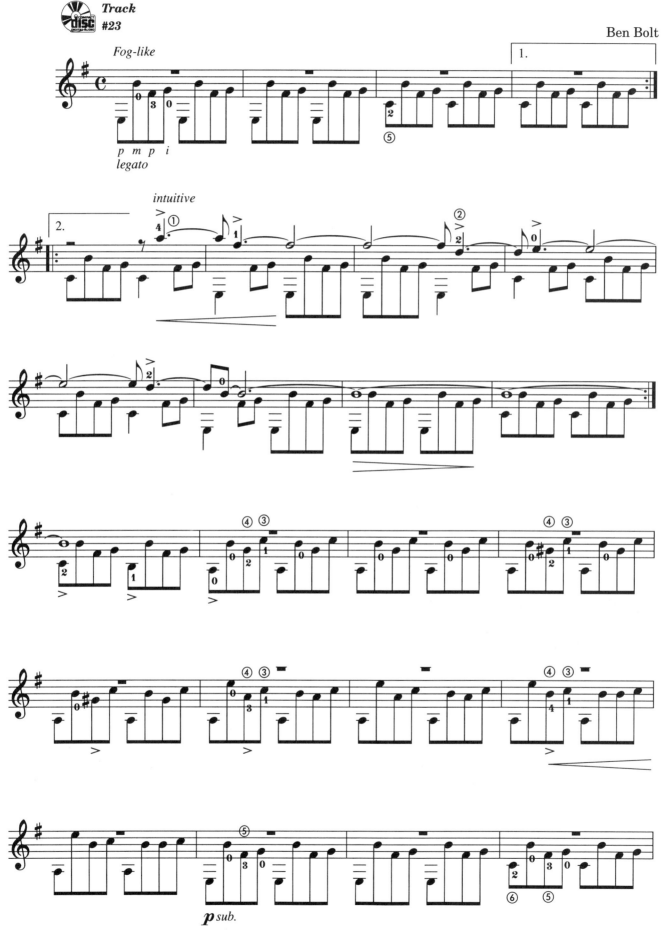

78

G MAJOR

Position Two

The key of G has one sharp (♯). All F notes will be raised one fret.

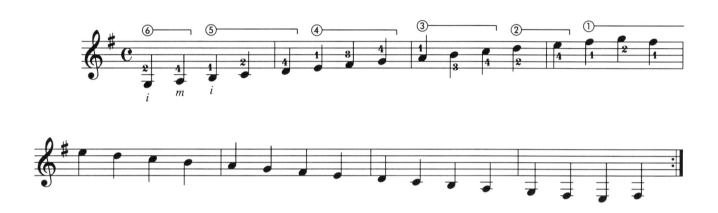

Position Seven

Make certain you alternate your right-hand fingers. The *Military Step* on page 58 can be used for any scale. Also, something I like to do is play each note three or four times each!

SPRING MORNING
To Michael Hedges

Ben Bolt

Track
#25

* Repeats not taken
in recording.

MARCH

P.I. Tchaikovsky

arr. Ben Bolt

* Look at page 86.

MARCH

* Repeats not taken
in recording.

Fernando Sor

arr. Ben Bolt

⌢ The fermata means hold the note longer.

ALLEGRETTO

Track #27

* Repeats not taken in recording.

M. Carcassi

arr. Ben Bolt

PINKY PIVOT

D Major Second Position

Track #28

Ben Bolt

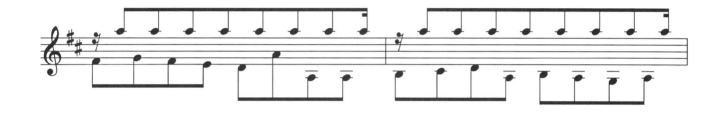

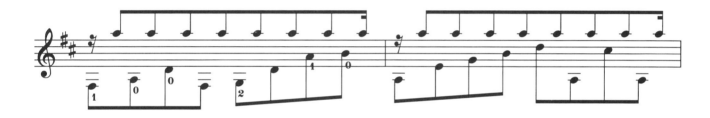

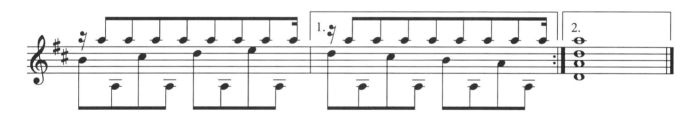

D SCALE IN TWO OCTAVES
Ninth Position

RIGHT-HAND HARMONICS

Steps   Touch, play, lift harmonics are done in one motion, like a wave. Add 12 frets to any note on the same string to create harmonics for any pitch. Place the tip of your index finger on top of the fret, not behind.

For bass notes play with your thumb.

AWAY IN A MANGER

Melody in Harmonics

arr. Ben Bolt

Track #29

87

ALLEGRO ALLA RENAISSANCE

arr. Ben Bolt

SALTARELLO

Melody with Bass Line

Track #31

arr. Ben Bolt

HARK, THE HERALD ANGELS SING

Felix Mendelssohn

arr. Ben Bolt

O LITTLE TOWN OF BETHLEHEM

Track #33

Lewis H. Redner

* Repeats not taken
in recording.

arr. Ben Bolt

⑥ = D

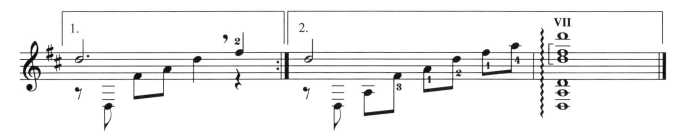

Track #34

*Repeats not taken in recording.

ALLEGRETTO

M. Carcassi

arr. Ben Bolt

92

HALLELUJAH CHORUS

arr. Ben Bolt

Track #35

G.F. Handel

94

95

A MAJOR

First and Second Positions

* transition to second position

The A Scale in 4ᵗʰ Position

The A Scale Alternating with an Open E String

Dominant Pedal E Note

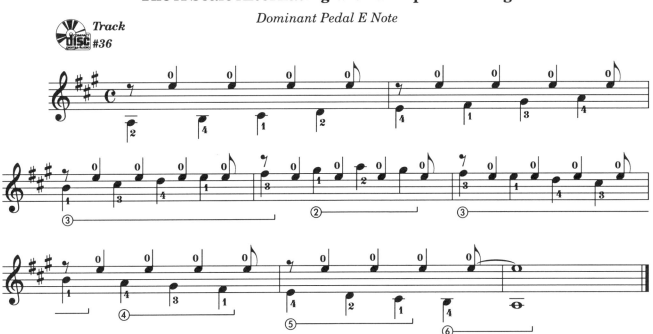

97

THE A MAJOR SCALE IN NINTH POSITION

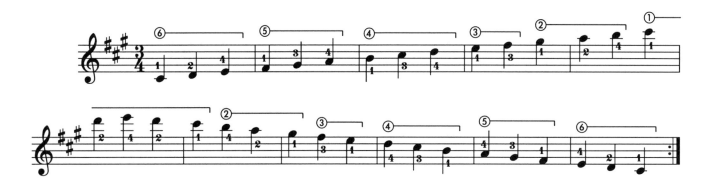

Pedal Notes

Pedal Notes are repeating notes that are tonic (first note in the scale) or dominant (fifth note in the scale). In A Major the tonic and dominant notes would be A and E respectively. The reason A is such a great key is because they just so happen to be open strings. This gives "FREEDOM" for other fingers to play more notes. In my next petite composition you will learn how effective Pedal Notes are. It will become clear why composers like Bach use them. Case in point, pedal tones recieved their name from the pedal notes of the organ.

DOMINANT PEDDLER
Parallel presentation, page 55

Track #37

Ben Bolt

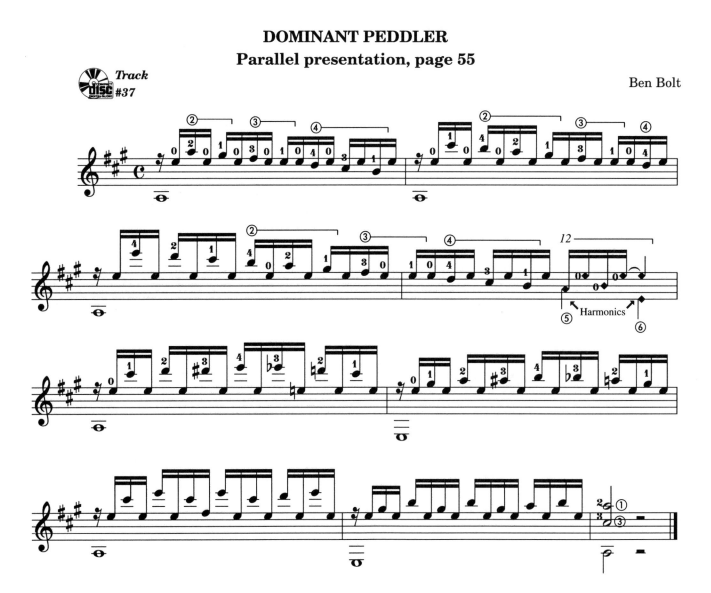

98

STUDY

* Repeats not taken
in recording.

F. Sor

arr. Ben Bolt

Rest your thumb on the fifth string for support.

PRELUDE IN A

To John Williams

Ben Bolt

ALLEGRETTO

Track #40

arr. Ben Bolt

M. Carcassi

ALLEGRETTO GRAZIOSO

Track #41

* Repeats not taken
in recording.

M. Carcassi

arr. Ben Bolt

102

PRELUDE IN E

arr. Ben Bolt

Track #42

F. Carulli

elbow close to your body

on the open A string your elbow
swings away from your body

keep second finger

your elbow swings toward
your body on the open B string
P.O.R. should be your second l.h. finger

elbow is now close to your body

SPOOF ON A FRENCH FOLK SONG
To Abel Carlevaro

Ben Bolt

Track #44

STUDY IN SIXTHS

* Repeats not taken in recording.

F. Sor

arr. Ben Bolt

108

CHROMATIC OCTAVES

E CHROMATIC SCALE

110

DIATONIC SCALES
Major and Minor

C major

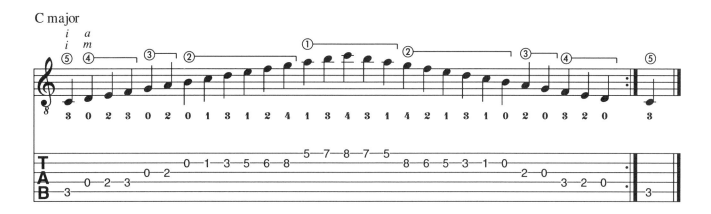

Db major

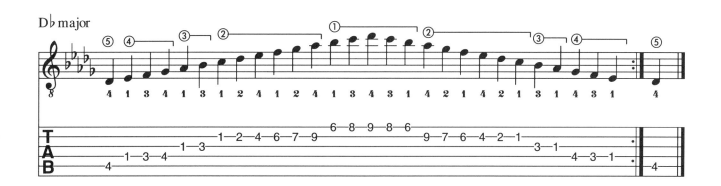

D major

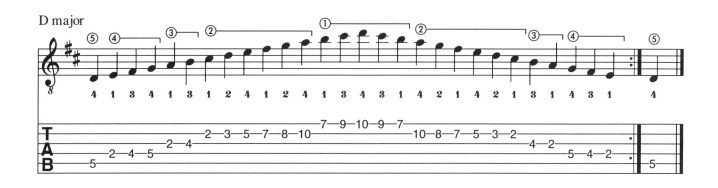

Eb major

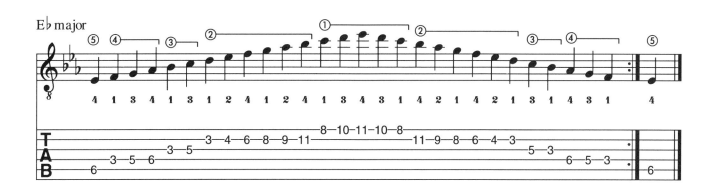

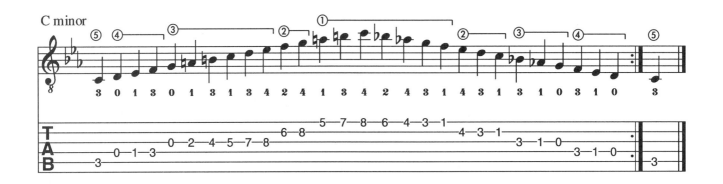

C minor

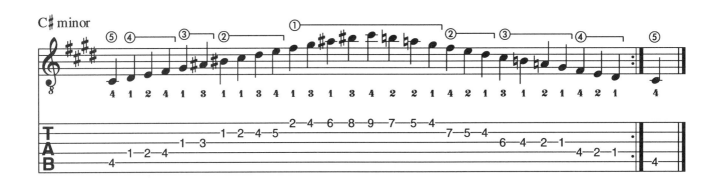

C♯ minor

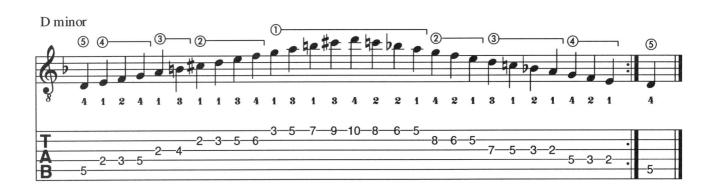

D minor

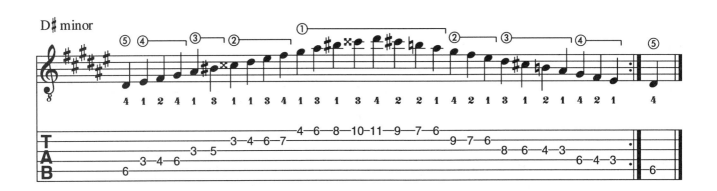

D♯ minor

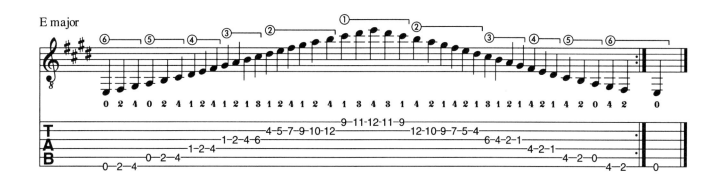

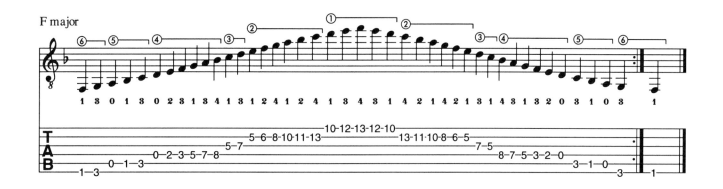

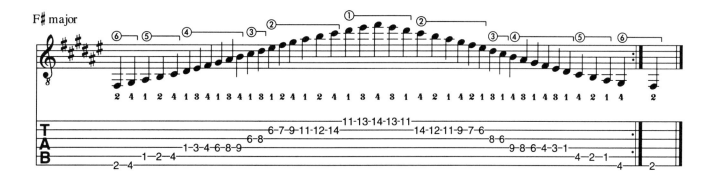

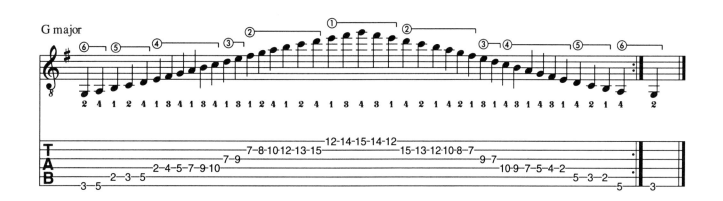

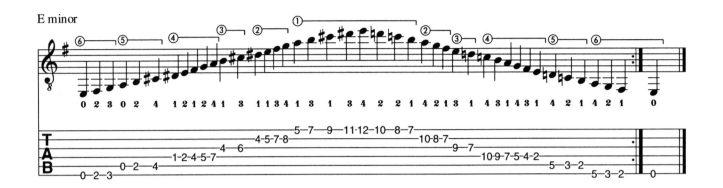

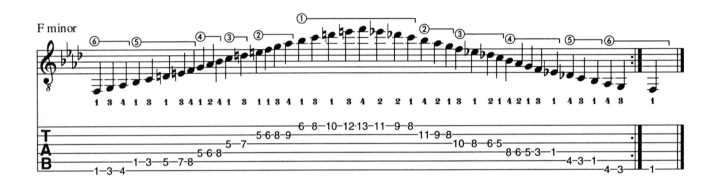

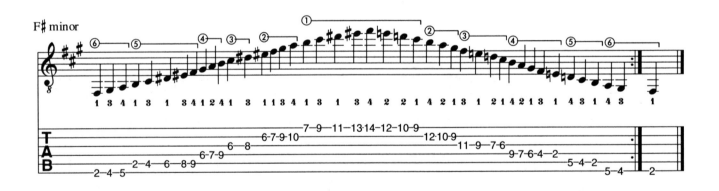

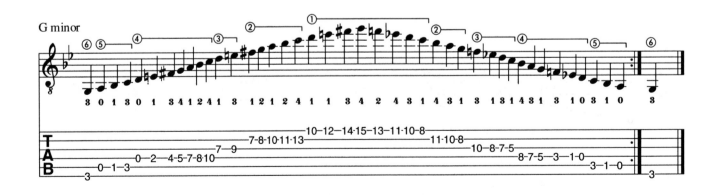

114

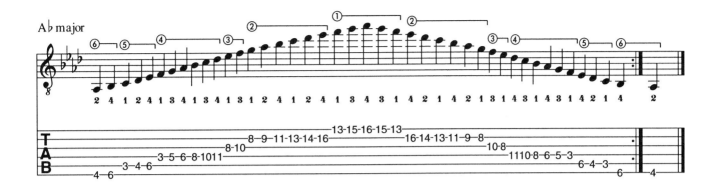

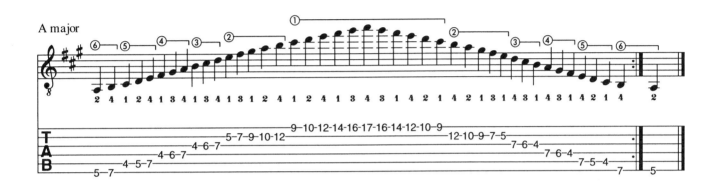

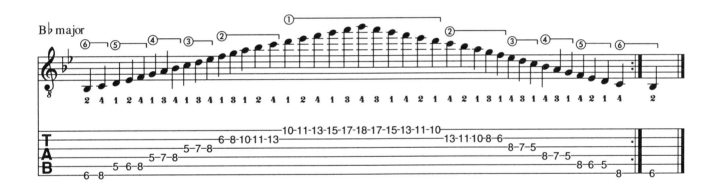

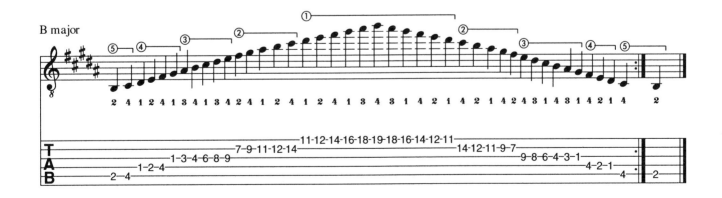

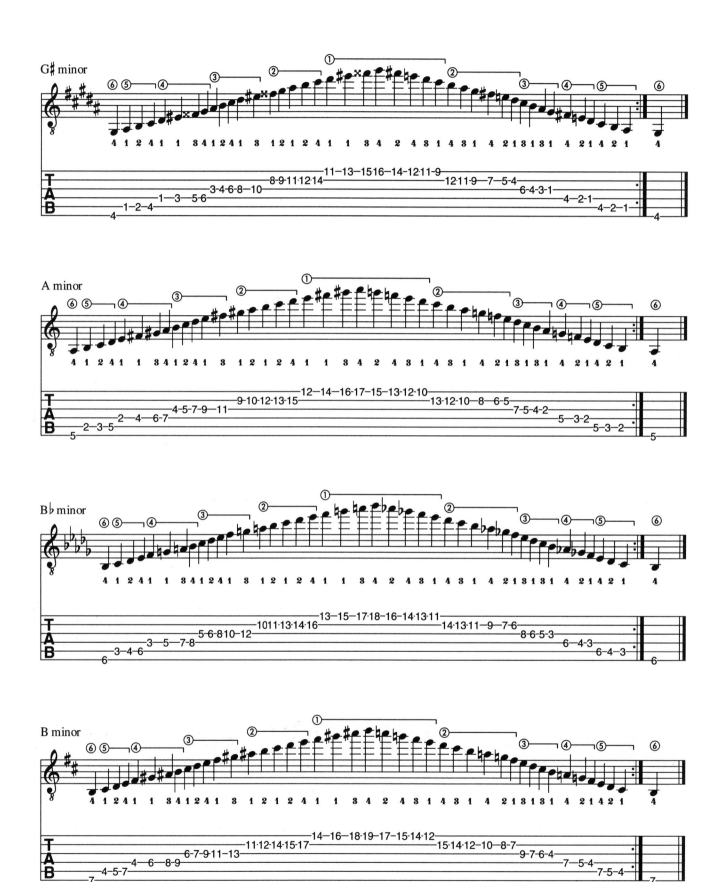

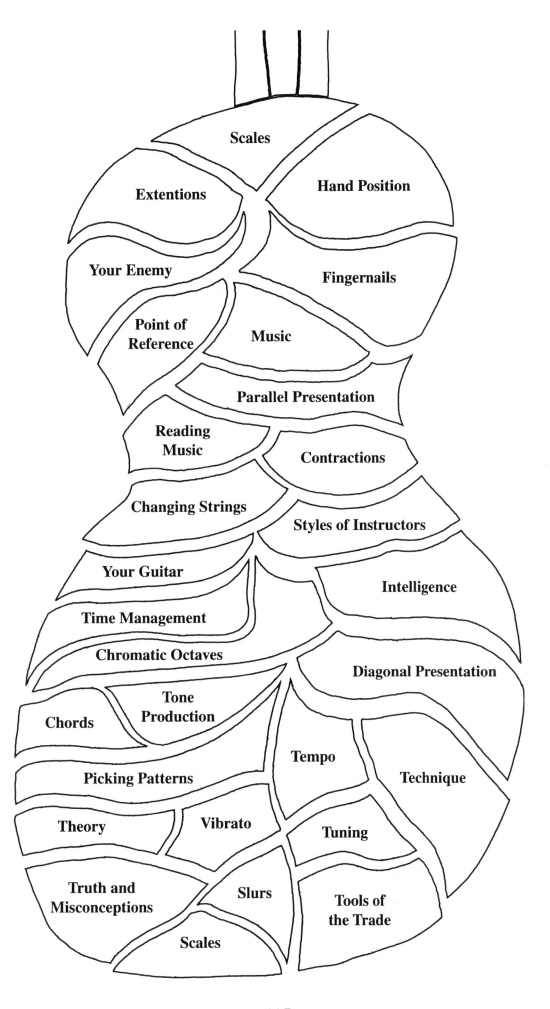

CLOSING COMMENTS FOR COMMITTED MUSICIANS ONLY

Music is recognized as one of the seven forms of human intelligence by Harvard Professor Dr. Howard Gardner, along with language, logic, visual, kinesthetic, interpersonal, and intrapersonal intelligence. Learning to play the guitar increases one's intelligence through exposure to a rich, stimulating environment.

Consider this: visual intelligence deals with imagination, visualization, design, shapes, and patterns. You need all of these things to play the guitar well. So you are thus developing your visual intelligence.

The kinesthetic relates to physical movement and expression through body language, physical exercise, drama, and dance. Have you ever seen a conductor of an orchestra when he really gets into it? It becomes almost like a dance. You'll need this skill too.

Musical intelligence relates to rhythmic and pitch intelligence, the effect of organized sound on the brain. Mozart must have had a brain like a computer. It's a fact that he would compose symphonies while playing billiards. And the original scores have no corrections! Clearly, he had remarkable musical intelligence.

Interpersonal intelligence relates to person to person encounters dealing with communication, working together toward a common goal and respecting, as well as noticing, distinctions among people. This refers to you and your teacher. The better it is, the more you'll learn.

Intrapersonal intelligence relates to knowing oneself. As a soloist, you will have to motivate yourself, deal with your good days and bad days, as well as juggle work or school and family responsibilities. Time management is such a personal juggling act. This could be the most important aspect of you becoming a great guitarist.

The mathematical component of logistics can be solving problems and analyzing fractions. For instance, if there are four beats in a measure, what are the variables that could be divided up (fractions) that would equate four equal beats? Four quarter notes or 16 16th notes or one whole note or two eight notes, a quarter note, four sixteen notes, and a quarter rest. This is logical problem solving that you will have to possess when you read and play music.

Lastly, verbal or linguistic intelligence includes humor, story telling, poetry, and verbal communication. If you are going to write a method one day, or if your destiny takes you to Spain and you need to learn a new language, you will be using your verbal intelligence. Music has been dubbed the international language, and rightfully so.

When you are in the presence of a great musician, you are in the presence of a highly intelligent person who uses all seven forms of human intelligence, often developed through desire and discipline. Don't ever let anyone make you feel inferior because you have chosen to be a musician.

Ben Bolt is credited with being the first classic guitar instructor to introduce the classic style of playing to the masses. Because of his worldwide success, his work has been mimicked throughout the publishing world. Several Ben Bolt books have consistently appeared on Mel Bay's "Best Seller" list. He also appears on Mel Bay's videos of the complete volumes of "The Modern Guitar Method", a huge commercial success, selling in the millions of copies. His publications are distributed internationally and have been featured at all the major conventions and music shows, including the National Association of Music Merchants in Germany. His video "Anyone Can Play the Classic Guitar" has become a reference for college students as the authority on the fundamentals of classic technique. He is endorsed by D'Addario Strings and Takamine Guitars. He has recorded the classic guitar work for HGTV and can be heard in the background of programs such as "America's Castles".

Ben Bolt first met Andres Segovia in the American Embassy in Madrid, Spain on his 18th birthday. Bolt was registering for the draft as Maestro Segovia was getting his Visa together to tour the U.S. This fortuitous meeting was the beginning of their relationship. Andres Segovia, the Father of the classic guitar, was quoted saying "Ben Bolt is an excellent guitarist with fine tone." After studying with Segovia, the Maestro personally paid for scholarships so that Bolt could continue his studies abroad, as well as setting up lessons with his assistants while he was on tour.

Ben Bolt first met Abel Carlevaro in Paris. Carlevaro then invited the 20 year old to study with him under full scholarship at the yearly Master Classes held in Brazil. After Brazil, Bolt moved to Montevideo, Uruguay. He won first place in the "Concurso Internacional Aemus" by unanimous decision. Carlevaro awarded him the coveted "Premio de Merito" at the National Library of Montevideo for his outstanding efforts in music. In 1978, Bolt assisted maestro Carlevaro in his first master's class in the states held at the San Francisco Conservatory of music. Bolt completed his music studies under the direction of Maestro Guido Santorsola, who bestowed him with an original composition for guitar entitled "Seis Bagatelas" as a graduation gift. After returning to the States he became the first guitarist inducted as a National Patron of Delta Omicron's International Music Fraternity.

EXCELLENCE IN MUSIC

MEL BAY®

Since 1947